Alien Invaders

Invasores Extraterrestres

Written by / Escrito por Lynn Huggins-Cooper
Illustrated by / Ilustrado por Bonnie Leick
Translated by / Traducido por Eida de la Vega

Huggins-Cooper, Lynn.

Alien invaders / written by Lynn Huggins-Cooper ; illustrated by Bonnie Leick ; translated by Eida de la Vega = Invasores extraterrestres / escrito por Lynn Huggins-Cooper ; ilustrado por Bonnie Leick ; traducción al español de Eida de la Vega. -- 1st ed. -- Green Bay, WI : Raven Tree Press, 2004.

p. ; cm.

Text in English and Spanish.

Summary: A child compares garden creatures to what he knows of space invaders. Bugs and creepy crawlers abound in far-out illustrations.

ISBN: 0972497390   ISBN: 0974199273 PB

1. Insects--Juvenile fiction. 2. Gardens--Juvenile fiction. 3. Imagination--Juvenile fiction. 4. Life on other planets--Juvenile fiction. 5. Bilingual books--English and Spanish. 6. [Spanish language materials--books.] I. Illust. Leick, Bonnie. II. Title. III. Invasores extraterrestres.

PZ7.H844 A45   2003109087
813.6 [E]--dc22   CIP

Printed in the U.S.A.

10 9 8 7 6 5 4 3 2 1
first edition

Alien Invaders

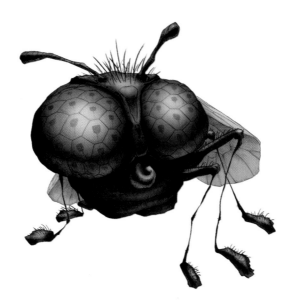

Invasores Extraterrestres

Written by / Escrito por Lynn Huggins-Cooper
Illustrated by / Ilustrado por Bonnie Leick
Translated by / Traducido por Eida de la Vega

Raven Tree Press LLC
www.raventreepress.com

I heard that aliens
are little green men.

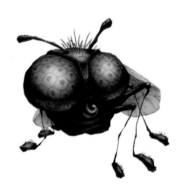

Yo he oído que los
extraterrestres
son hombrecitos verdes.

Wrong!
The alien invaders
are here.

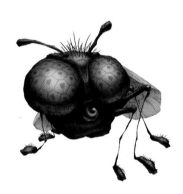

¡Nada de eso!
Los invasores
extraterrestres
ya están aquí.

They set up camp
in our garden.

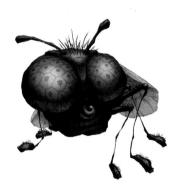

Están levantando
un campamento
en nuestro jardín.

They have robot legs.
They wear shiny
suits and helmets.

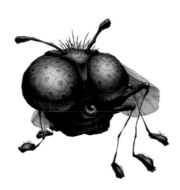

Tienen patas de robot.

Usan trajes y
cascos brillantes.

They watch us with camera lens eyes.

Are they taking pictures?

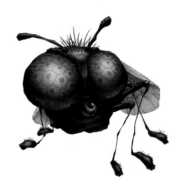

Nos observan con ojos que parecen cámaras fotográficas.

¿Estarán tomando fotos?

Some fly and dive.

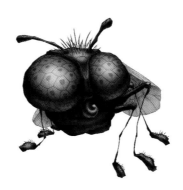

Algunos vuelan y bajan en picado.

Others slither.

They leave clues.

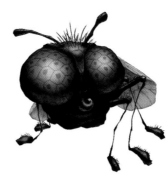

Otros se mueven como serpientes y van dejando un rastro a su paso.

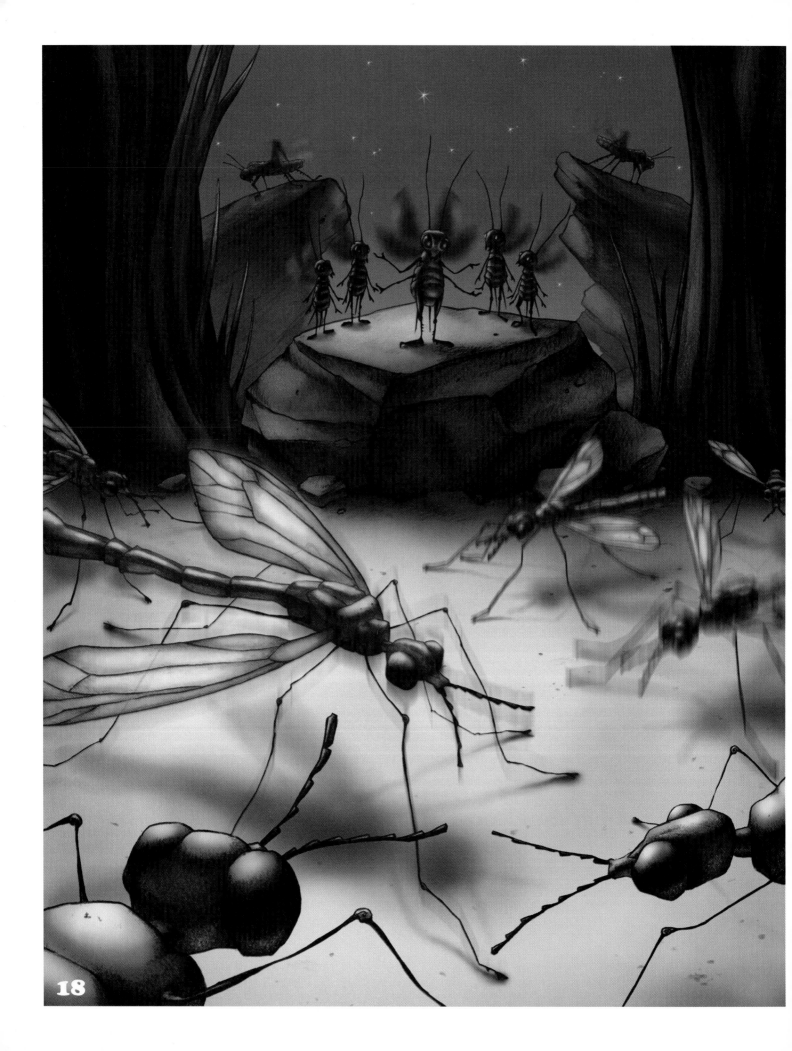

I hear them whisper
in secret languages.

I see them dance
strange dances.

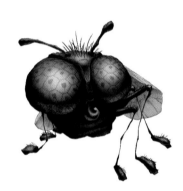

Los escucho hablar bajito
en lenguas secretas.

Los veo bailar bailes
extraños.

They build cities under our feet

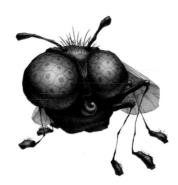

Construyen ciudades bajo nuestros pies

and spin
dangerous traps.

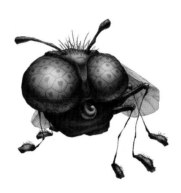

y tejen
trampas peligrosas.

They sneak
into our houses
and watch us.

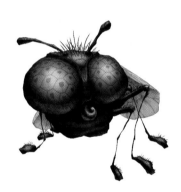

**Entran a escondidas
en nuestras casas
y nos observan.**

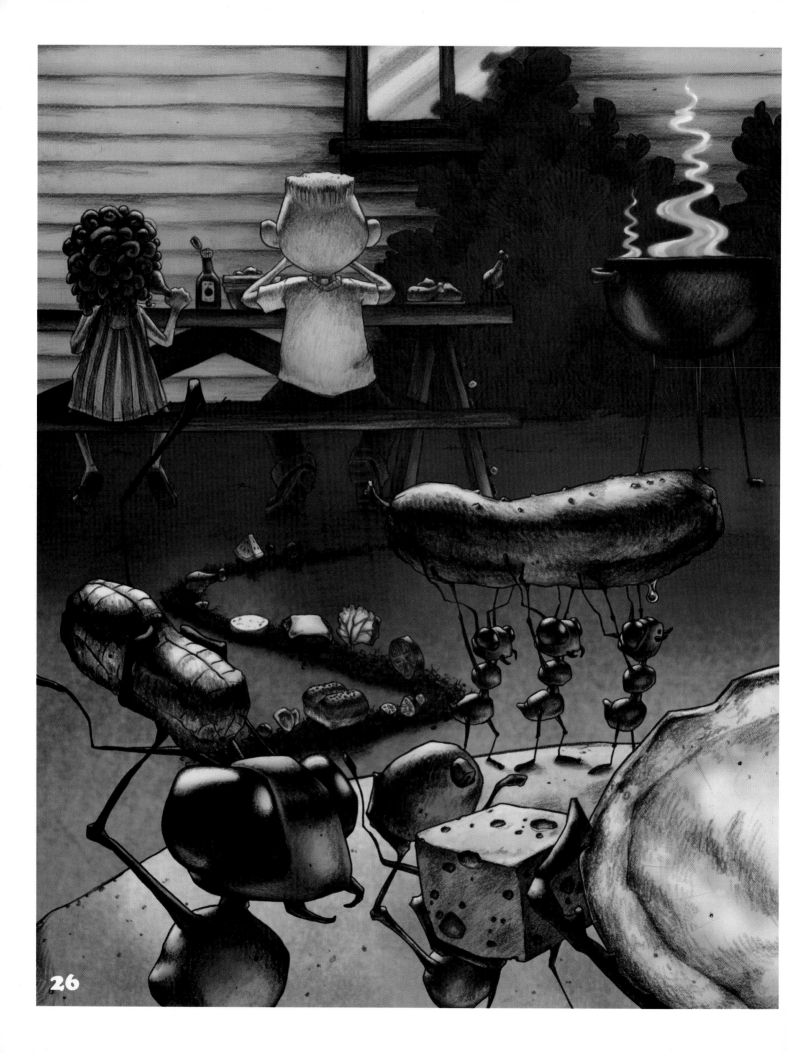

There are many more of them than us.

Son muchos más que nosotros.

27

Mom says they are
just bugs.

But I am making
friends with them,
just in case.

Mamá dice que sólo
son insectos, pero
por si acaso,
me estoy haciendo
amigo de ellos.

They sure look
like aliens to me!

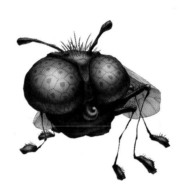

¡A mí me parecen
extraterrestres!

Vocabulary

Vocabulario

Singular	Plural	Singular	Plural
bug	bugs	insecto	insectos
camp	camps	campamento	campamentos
garden	gardens	jardín	jardines
friend	friends	amigo	amigos
picture	pictures	foto	fotos
eye	eyes	ojo	ojos
snake	snakes	serpiente	serpientes
clue	clues	rastro	rastros
dance	dances	baile	bailes
city	cities	ciudad	ciudades
house	houses	casa	casas
leg	legs	pata	patas